GIRLS
TO THE
RESCUE

*Tales of clever, courageous girls
from around the world*

EDITED BY BRUCE LANSKY

Meadowbrook Press

Distributed by Simon & Schuster
New York

Library of Congress Cataloging-in-Publication Data

Girls to the rescue: tales of clever, courageous girls from around
the world/selected by Bruce Lansky.
p. cm.
Contents: The fairy godmother's assistant—Grandma Rosa's bowl—For love
of Sunny—Carla and the greedy merchant—Savannah's piglets—Kimi meets the
ogre—The innkeeper's wise daughter—The royal joust—Chardae's thousand
and one nights—Lian and the unicorn.
Summary: A collection of ten stories featuring admirable girls in both familiar
and exotic settings.
ISBN: 0-88166-215-1 (pbk.)
1. Children's stories. [1. Short stories] I. Lansky, Bruce.
PZ5.G447   1995
[Fic]—dc20   95-17733

Simon & Schuster Ordering # 0-671-89979-1

All the stories are copyrighted and published with the permission of the authors.

pp. 1, 17, and 69 "The Fairy Godmother's Assistant," "Grandma Rosa's Bowl," and "The
Royal Joust" © 1995 by Bruce Lansky; pp. 23 and 95 "For Love of Sunny" © 1984 and
"Lian and the Unicorn" © 1995 by Vivian Vande Velde. Original version of "For Love
of Sunny" first appeared in *Once Upon a Test: Three Light Tales of Love* by Vivian Vande
Velde (Albert Whitman & Co., 1984); p. 33 "Carla and the Greedy Merchant" © 1995
by Robert Scotellaro; p. 39 "Savannah's Piglets" © 1995 by Sheryl Nelms; p. 51 "Kimi
Meets the Ogre" © 1995 by Linda Cave; p. 61 "The Innkeeper's Wise Daughter" © 1987
by Peninnah Schram. Original version first appeared in *Jewish Stories One Generation
Tells Another* by Peninnah Schram (Jason Aronson Inc., Northvale, NJ., 1987); p. 81
"Chardae's Thousand and One Nights" © 1995 by Craig Hansen.

Published by Meadowbrook Press, 5451 Smetana Drive, Minnetonka, MN 55343

BOOK TRADE DISTRIBUTION by Simon & Schuster, a division of
Simon and Schuster, Inc., 1230 Avenue of the Americas, New York, NY 10020

Editor: Bruce Lansky
Editorial Coordinator: Liya Lev Oertel
Production Manager: Amy Unger
Desktop Publishing Manager: Patrick Gross
Graphic Designer: Linda Norton
Art Coordinator: Erik Broberg
Cover Illustration: Gay Holland

05 04 03 02 01   15 14 13 12 11

Printed in the United States of America

Dedication

I dedicate this book to my daughter, Dana, and to all daughters.

When Dana was a child I used to make up bedtime stories in which she was the hero. You see, Lady Dana was one of the smartest and bravest of all of the knights of the Round Table in Camelot. King Arthur would ask her advice and help when problems arose. She could always come up with a way to rescue the kingdom from whatever peril threatened—usually with a creative approach that never would have occurred to knights whose favorite solution is fighting. (I'd usually ask her, "And what do you think Lady Dana did?" and incorporate her suggestion into the story.)

I was hoping that these stories would give Dana the confidence to set ambitious goals, and then accomplish them. I'm happy to say that, so far, she's well on her way toward making her dreams come true. I'm very proud of her.

My hope is that these stories will have the same effect on all daughters that my bedtime stories had on Dana.

Acknowledgements

We would like to thank the young women
who served on a reading panel for this project:
Dana Almer, Michelle Barnes, Heidi Behruns, Lynsey Bergeron,
Laura Bohen, Connie Bottenberg, Kelly Bottenberg,
Natasha Bruggeman, Anna Burk, Elissa Burk, Kelsey Campbell,
Cara Chamberlain, Chelsea Cohr, Katie Comstock,
Megan Djerf, Stephanie Djerf, Kalena Ferdig, Lizzie Flannigan,
Annie Fredrickson, Liza Getsinger, Kathryn Gilbertson,
Carla Granger, Jennifer Lynn Gruenhagen, Sydney Hanson,
Catherine Henderson, Kimberly Hicks, Katy Hinton,
Kamalar Howard, Sarah Johns, Jessie Johnson, Melissa Jones,
Kayla Koep, Kashena Jade Konecki, Angelina Kostreba,
Diana Kruppstadt, Christine Lamb, Leah Lehmkuhl,
Kristi Lund, Kari Melchert, Lauren Mueller, Nancy Muldor,
Gina Patterson, Bobbie Peterson, Sarah Popkin, Lauren Rath,
Stephanie Reichel, Claire Reuning, Kim Ricci, Michelle Roers,
Julie Rogers, Samantha Schwartz, Mindy Spencer,
Leah Steinberg, Betsy Steiner, Sharon Swearington,
Alexa Textor, Natasha Uspensky, Michelle Verant,
Angela Wagner, Betsy Waalen, Catherine Wicks, Sarah Wiita,
Amy Xiong, Hanna Zipes

Contents

Introduction

If you're curious about why I decided to collect and write stories about clever, courageous girls, I can rattle off five good reasons: "Cinderella," "Snow White," "Sleeping Beauty," "Rapunzel," and "The Princess and the Pea."

These fairy tales were written one hundred and fifty to two hundred years ago—before most princes had joined the ranks of the unemployed, and before women had landed jobs as rocket scientists, brain surgeons, and VJs on MTV.

But some people just don't get that the whole premise of these stories is as obsolete as the horse-drawn carriage. Think about it:

• Cinderella can't figure out how to get to the ball without magical help from her fairy godmother. And she can't get back home without losing one of her shoes. A handsome prince returns the shoe and marries her. They live happily ever after.

• Snow White keeps falling for her stepmother's dumb dirty tricks. She eats a poisoned apple and falls into a coma. Then Prince Charming wakes her up with a kiss and rides off with her on the back of his horse. They marry and live happily ever after.

• Sleeping Beauty doesn't do much but sleep for a hundred years. Then a handsome prince, who must have read "Snow

White," wakes her with a kiss and marries her. They live happily ever after.

• Rapunzel lives in a tower, where she does nothing but mope and grow long hair. A handsome prince climbs the tower and rescues her. They marry and live happily ever after.

• A persnickety princess complains that she couldn't sleep a wink on a bed with twenty mattresses because the bed was too lumpy. A pea had been put under all the mattresses to test whether she was a true princess. A handsome prince proposes to Princess Grumpy on the spot. They marry and live happily every after.

But you understand that there's more to life than waiting around for a handsome prince, that singing "Someday my prince will come" in the shower is a big waste of water, and that life doesn't always turn out "happily ever after." Princess Di and Princess Fergy learned this lesson the hard way!

Because you understand what these fairy tales are all about, you are ready for something new. The stories I've collected in *Girls to the Rescue* are very different from traditional fairy tales in a number of ways:

First, the heroes of these stories are girls and young women—not princes or fairy godmothers.

Second, the heroes succeed because they are clever, courageous, and kind. They don't rely on their beauty. They don't rely on magic. They don't resort to violence.

Third, most of the stories are about helping families,

friends, and country—not about getting married. Two stories that do deal with marriage don't treat it as the ultimate goal. Instead, they focus mainly on love and respect within marriage.

Fourth, many of the stories feature surprising twists on traditional themes. They were written by a number of different writers, so the styles vary: some are humorous, some are adventurous, some are romantic, and some are noble.

Fifth, the stories are set in countries all around the world. You'll meet characters from Mexico, Ireland, Russia, Japan, China, Persia, and the American frontier as well as from England and Germany.

I hope that you enjoy them so much you'll want to share them. I also hope you are motivated to think about how you, like the heroes in this book, can help your family, friends, and country.

Bruce Lansky

The Fairy Godmother's Assistant

AN ORIGINAL STORY BY BRUCE LANSKY

When you need help, don't you wish a fairy god-mother would suddenly appear to make things right? Well, don't hold your breath. She doesn't do that kind of thing anymore. (She's getting on in years, you know.) So if you want some help—she still fixes anything from broken windows to broken hearts—you'll have to visit her little cottage in the Bavarian woods and wait your turn, just like everyone else. And when you knock on the door, I'll let you in and make you comfortable. I'll even serve you a nice cold glass of lemonade.

You see, I'm the fairy godmother's assistant.

My job used to be quite simple, really, until the fairy godmother announced she would be taking a much-needed vacation. I was scared stiff! What would I say to people who came for help? I didn't know any magic. I couldn't have turned a pumpkin into a glittering coach if my life depended on it.

"Don't worry," the fairy godmother told me. "You're very sensible. I'm sure you'll find a way to handle whatever comes up. And besides, I'll only be gone for a few days."

To be honest, I didn't get much sleep that night. I kept wondering how I could possibly fill her shoes.

I got up early the next morning and went to the kitchen to make a fresh pitcher of lemonade. When I heard a knock at the door, I opened it and found a young woman with a tear-stained face, wearing a tattered old dress. I explained that the fairy godmother would be gone for a few days and that I was her assistant. But she looked so sad that I invited her in for a glass of lemonade to cheer her up.

As soon as she sat down, she started to cry. I sat beside her and gave her a handkerchief to dry her eyes. "First wipe away your tears. Then tell me what's bothering you," I said in a soothing voice.

The young woman took a few deep breaths before speaking. "My name is Ella, but my stepmother and stepsisters call me Cinder-Ella, because my apron is always covered with cinders from cleaning the fire-place. They are mean to me and make me clean the house, cook, sew, and run errands all day while they have fun. Now I have to make them new gowns for the royal ball. But I want to go, too." She started to cry again.

I could guess where this was leading. "I'm very sorry to hear that," I responded. "I suppose you came to ask the fairy godmother to get you to the ball. Is that it?"

She nodded.

"I wish I could help you, but I make lemonade not magic."

Ella began to cry again. "Can't you do anything?"

"There's not much I can do. It's really up to you."

She dried her eyes again with the handkerchief and stared at me in amazement. "Up to me?" she queried.

"It's really very simple," I said. "If you want to go to the ball, go. And don't let anything or anyone stop you."

"But how can I go to the ball without an evening gown?"

"Don't look at me," I responded. "You're the seamstress. If you can make gowns for your two stepsisters, why not make another for yourself?"

Ella pondered this for awhile, then shook her head. "But I can't afford to buy silk or velvet. How can I make a gown without any fabric?"

"Are there any velvet curtains in your house? Or silk bed sheets?"

Her worried look slowly turned into a smile. "There sure are!" she gushed. But her smile was short-lived. Another question had flashed into her mind. "But what about dancing slippers? I don't have any."

"Then don't wear any," I advised.

Ella couldn't believe her ears. "You mean I should go to the royal ball barefooted?"

"What choice do you have, unless you want to wear those ugly boots you're wearing?"

"And how am I supposed to get to the ball?" she asked. This young woman certainly could think up problems! "The royal palace is almost a mile from my house."

I knew Ella wouldn't like my answer. "I suppose you'll just have to walk."

A big frown appeared on her face. This wasn't the kind of help she had hoped to get from her fairy godmother. "But they'll never let me in if I don't arrive in a fancy, horse-drawn carriage," she whined.

"You're right," I agreed. "They may not let you in through the main gate, but I don't think there's anyone guarding the door to the kitchen. Do you?"

"I guess not," she said tentatively. "At least I hope not!"

Ella seemed uncomfortable with my answers. She'd never done anything quite so daring before. I wasn't surprised when I heard another "but."

"But if a prince asks me to dance, what should I say?"

"Ask him to be careful not to step on your toes," I joked.

Ella laughed so hard, she had to use the handkerchief again. Sensing she was close to deciding in favor of going to the ball, I gave her one more push. "What have you got to lose?"

"Nothing!" Ella exclaimed, smiling from ear to ear. "Nothing at all!"

She stood up to shake my hand. "Thank you for all your help. I've got to go now. I've got so many things to do!"

Before she left, I offered her some final advice. "If you don't want your stepmother and stepsisters to know you've been to the ball, be sure to leave by twelve o'clock sharp. That way you'll be back in bed by the time they get home."

I was quite pleased with myself for helping Ella. Relaxing for a moment with a glass of lemonade, I wondered if the fairy godmother with all her magic could have done a better job. I spent a good part of the day congratulating myself and feeling thankful I'd gotten through my first problem without messing up.

After dinner, I was surprised by a knock at the door. When I opened it, I discovered a distinguished-looking elderly gentleman. He looked ever-so-much like the king, as pictured on every postage stamp in Bavaria, except that this man looked older, frailer, and far more worried. He must have been trying to keep his visit a secret; no guards or footmen were with him. I curtsied deeply as soon as I let him in.

"Enough of that," he blustered. "I must see the fairy godmother at once!"

"I'm sorry, Your Highness," I explained. "She's away. Can I help you?"

"Perhaps," he replied. "Do you know where she keeps her magic potions?"

"If you tell me which potion you'd like, I'll be happy to look," I said in as helpful a voice as I could muster.

The king looked embarrassed. "Well, actually, I'm looking for a potion that would enable me to, well … live forever."

I offered the king a comfortable chair, excused myself, and went to the cabinet where the fairy godmother kept her potions. In a short time I returned with a handful of bottles. "I've found a potion to keep your breath fresh longer, and one to make your suntan last longer. But I can't find anything to help you live longer, not even for a day."

His royal highness was definitely not overjoyed by this news. "In that case, I'll wait here till the fairy godmother returns. You see, I'm not feeling well, and the royal doctors haven't been much use."

"I'm sorry to hear that, Your Highness. What seems to be the problem?"

"My back, for one thing. It's killing me. And I can't sleep at night because of terrible gas pains, not to mention splitting headaches. My eyesight's growing dim. I'm deaf in one ear. I'm growing forgetful … or did I mention that already? But worst of all, my twin sons are driving me crazy! Aside from that, I'm fine—just fine." There was no mistaking his sarcastic tone.

"I think you must be terribly uncomfortable, Your Highness. But why would you want to live forever? Surely your health will continue to get worse as you grow older. In a few years, you'll be confined to bed. Would you enjoy living forever in bed?"

"I never thought of it that way," he admitted thoughtfully. "But at least if I lived forever I wouldn't have to worry about how to divide the kingdom between my sons, Prince Sherman and Prince Herman. They're identical twins, you know. Even I can't tell them apart! You see, no matter how I divide it, one or both of them will be angry with me. Their squabbling is driving me crazy … or did I mention that already?" he asked absent-mindedly.

"Your memory serves you well," I answered diplomatically. "But I wonder, if two sons' squabbling is driving you crazy, how will you like it when you have eight grandchildren arguing over how to divide the kingdom? Or thirty-two great-grandchildren? Or a hundred-and-twenty-eight great-great-grandchildren? If you're not crazy yet, that should do it."

The king appeared lost in thought. "Come to think of it," he answered, "the longer I put off making a decision, the worse it will get. I suppose I'll have to make the best of my situation for as long as I can. You've been more helpful than you can imagine. I'm glad the fairy godmother was away."

With more energy than he'd displayed since he arrived, he got up from his chair and announced, "I must be on my way."

He smiled as though a great burden had been lifted from his back.

He headed for the door, opened it, and was almost gone when he turned and said, "I want you to forget I was ever here ... or did I mention that already?"

He reached into his pocket and pulled out a bag of gold coins, which he handed me. He didn't see me collapse into the armchair and pull out a handkerchief to wipe my face. This had been a most unusual day, and I was anxious to relax in a tub full of hot water and bubbles. (I'd found an excellent bubble bath in the fairy godmother's potion cabinet.)

The next morning was uneventful. I'd slept well and was ready for anything. Then, around noon, "anything" happened. Who do you think knocked at the fairy godmother's door just as I was starting to think about lunch? Prince Sherman and Prince Herman!

The first thing I noticed when I let them in was how angry they looked. They were arguing about something on the doorstep, and they continued to argue as I opened the door.

"I want the horses and the stables so I can play polo," said Prince Sherman. (I could tell he was Sherman because he had a large "S" monogrammed on his tunic.)

"No way," replied Prince Herman. (He was the one with a large "H" monogrammed on his tunic.) "I like to ride, too."

"Excuse me, Your Highnesses," I said as I curtsied.

"I'm afraid the fairy godmother isn't here. I'm her assistant."

"That's all right," said Prince Sherman. "Our father, the king, sent us to see you."

I couldn't believe my ears. "He sent you to see me?"

"That's right," said Prince Herman. "You see, he told us he's very sick and doesn't have long to live. And he said we'd have to figure out how to divide up the kingdom ourselves."

"And," Prince Sherman continued, "he said if we couldn't figure it out, to come and see you. Which is why we're here."

"What do you expect me to do?" I asked. "You know, I'm just the fairy godmother's assistant. I don't do magic."

"We know all that," said Prince Herman. "But father said what you do is better than magic."

I was surprised ... no, stunned ... no, shocked! "I- I- I'm fl- fl- flattered," I stammered, not knowing what else to say.

"So we'd like you to divide up the kingdom for us," they said in unison.

"I don't suppose I can refuse a royal command," I said hesitantly.

"What do you mean?" asked Prince Sherman suspiciously.

"You see, if I decide how to divide the royal kingdom, then you'll both be mad at me, because I can't possibly make you both happy. But I do have a couple of suggestions."

"Such as?" they demanded.

I cleared my throat to create some drama. "Ahem!"

"Yes?" they asked, waiting for a brilliant pronouncement.

"Well, you could both renounce the throne and let your cousin Fritz rule."

The twins looked at each other, wondering whether the other would seriously consider such a proposal. "Nah!" they said simultaneously.

"Or you could share the throne and rule together."

"Impossible!" exclaimed Prince Sherman.

"Disastrous!" proclaimed Prince Herman.

"We can't agree about anything," added Prince Sherman. He paused, "Well, almost anything. We both agree that's a stupid idea."

"Then there's only one option." Again I paused for dramatic effect. "Prince Sherman, you divide the kingdom as evenly as you can. Prince Herman, you choose which half you want."

Prince Sherman looked at Prince Herman. Prince Herman looked at Prince Sherman. They smiled. Then they looked at me. Still smiling, they both reached into their pockets, pulled out bags of gold coins, and handed them to me at the same time. Then they walked out the door with their arms on each other's shoulders. They barely made it through the door.

"I can't believe it!" I said to no one in particular as soon as I'd collapsed into the armchair again. Thank goodness there were no more visitors that day. I'd had all the excitement I could handle.

That night over dinner, I wondered whether Ella ever went to the royal ball. The next day I found out. Just before noon she knocked on the front door. She was carrying a satchel and looking tired but happy. I was about to ask, "How was the ball?" but she started talking before I could say a word.

"The ball was great! The music! The food! The dancing! Everything! I would never have gone without your help!" she gushed.

"Thanks," I replied. "But I can't take any credit. You did it all yourself. By the way, what's in your satchel?"

"All my belongings," Ella replied. "After attending the royal ball, I really couldn't go back to living with my stepmother and stepsisters. So I decided to move to town and open up a dressmaker's shop. I really am a good seamstress, you know.

"I just came by to thank you and to tell you the latest news from court. Last night, the king announced he was stepping down from the throne so he can travel. He turned the throne over to Prince Herman—all except the stables. Apparently, Prince Sherman has decided to devote himself to polo."

As she was leaving, I said, "I'd like to be your first customer. I'll be in to see you for a fitting next week."

"Thanks," she said. "Maybe we can go to the royal ball together next year."

"I'd love to," I replied. "But next year we'll go in style. We'll rent a coach for the evening. And we'll both wear dancing slippers, too." Ella walked out the door laughing.

The fairy godmother returned the next day. She didn't seem surprised when I told her all the things that had occurred while she was away. "I told you when I left that you could handle whatever came up," she said.

I wonder if those were magic words.

Grandma Rosa's Bowl

ADAPTED BY BRUCE LANSKY FROM A GRIMM BROTHERS' STORY

While visiting a poor village in Mexico, I stopped in an antique shop and picked up a dusty old diary.

The shopkeeper told me that it had belonged to a girl named Maria, who had lived nearby with her mother, Sevilla, many years ago. I hope she will not mind if I share her story with you.

Maria's father had died when she was young, so her mother worked very hard as a potter to make a modest living. When Maria's father's mother became too old and frail to take care of herself, she had no alternative but to move into the little house of Maria and her mother.

From the very first day, Maria enjoyed Grandma Rosa's company. While Sevilla worked at the potter's wheel, Grandma Rosa made herself useful by mending clothes. But because her eyes were weak and her hands trembled, putting the thread through the tiny eye of the needle was very hard for her. So Maria helped her grandmother thread the needle and was rewarded with fascinating stories about her father when he was a boy.

Sevilla was worried about making ends meet now that there was one more mouth to feed. The first night at the dinner table, when Grandma Rosa spilled some soup, Sevilla got angry. "You should be more careful," she warned. "I work hard to put food on the table."

The next night, when Grandma Rosa dropped a dinner bowl on the floor, Sevilla became even angrier. "That beautiful dinner bowl would have brought ten pesos in the market. Now it is broken. You are too clumsy to eat from my best pottery. Here is a plain clay bowl. Eat from that."

The very next night at dinner when Grandma Rosa spilled her coffee on the rug, Sevilla lost her temper.

"*¡Ay, caramba!*" she yelled. "First you waste my good soup, then you break my beautiful bowl, and now you stain my carpet. You are too clumsy to eat with us in the dining room." Sevilla set up a little table on the front porch, where Grandma Rosa finished her dinner.

After dinner Grandma Rosa went to her room with her head hanging down. When the old woman was getting ready to go to sleep, Maria came to her bedside to comfort her. The girl whispered to her grandmother, "I'm very sorry about the way my mother treated you. I know your feelings are hurt. I've thought of a way to help you: Tomorrow night at dinner, I want you to drop your bowl again."

"I do not understand," answered Grandma Rosa in a low voice. "If I drop my bowl, your mother will get upset and yell at me again."

"She may get angry, but don't worry," whispered Maria. "Everything will work out. You'll see."

The following night at dinner, Maria and Sevilla heard a loud crash on the porch. When Sevilla rushed out to see what had happened, she found that Grandma Rosa had dropped her clay bowl, and it had broken into several pieces.

"You are so clumsy!" she scolded. "Pick up the pieces and glue them back together. I'm not giving you another bowl to break."

Grandma Rosa's eyes filled with tears. Maria helped her grandmother up from the table and guided the frail woman to her room.

Then Maria returned to the porch and picked up the pieces of the broken bowl.

Later on that evening, Sevilla found Maria gluing the pieces of Grandma Rosa's broken bowl together. "How nice of you to fix Grandmother's bowl for her," Sevilla said.

"You are mistaken, Mama," answered Maria. "Tomorrow I am going to make a beautiful dinner bowl for Grandma Rosa. This glued-together bowl I will save. Many years from now, when you are as old and frail as Grandma Rosa, I will give it to you."

Now Sevilla's eyes filled with tears. She wept because she felt ashamed of the way she had treated her mother-in-law. And she wept because she was proud of Maria for having the wisdom and the courage to show her the error of her ways.

As soon as Sevilla's tears had dried, she went to Grandma Rosa and begged to be forgiven.

The next day, when dinner was served, Grandma Rosa was again seated at the dinner table. Unfortunately, while stirring sugar into her coffee, she knocked the sugar bowl onto the floor.

Sevilla looked down at the broken sugar bowl. She looked at the sugar that had spilled on the floor. Then she looked at Grandma Rosa and smiled. "Don't worry, Mama. Accidents sometimes happen. Enjoy your dinner."

And that was the first of many happy meals Maria's family enjoyed together from that time forward.

For Love of Sunny

AN ORIGINAL STORY BY VIVIAN VANDE VELDE

Once upon a time, when dragons and trolls roamed the earth, the king of a small country on an island now known as Ireland invited the royalty from neighboring kingdoms to a ball at his palace.

Two of the people who met at that ball were Princess Meghan and Prince Sean, who was called Sunny because of his cheerful smile. Before the ball had ended, the two had fallen in love.

But when Sunny brought the princess home to meet his mother, things didn't go well.

"This is Princess Meghan," Sunny started. "Her parents are—"

"I passed through her parents' land last year," the queen said. "A nasty little kingdom whose most interesting inhabitants are the reindeer. Her parents keep pigs in their living room, you know."

Meghan forced herself to smile politely. She explained, "We let the pigs inside when it was cold so they wouldn't freeze to death." A bit peeved, she added, "They didn't stay in the living room, you know."

Sunny shrugged. "Anyway, we want to get married."

"Fine," his mother said. "As soon as she passes the tests."

"What tests?" the princess asked somewhat warily.

"You have to kill the giant troll that lives in the valley and the dragon that lives on the mountain. And then ... let's see ... you have to answer three questions."

"But that's not fair!" Meghan cried. "I have never heard of a princess having to win the hand of a prince."

"We have the rule," the queen purred, "to make sure our prince marries someone worthy of him."

"Wait a minute," Sunny said. "I don't remember hearing about this rule last year, when you wanted me to marry the royal chancellor's daughter."

"The rule applies only to foreign-born princesses." The queen smiled. "Good day."

Meghan waited until the queen left, then said, "What kind of questions, I wonder? I'm not good at riddles, and I'm even worse at history. I don't mind doing all the dangerous stuff, but I'd hate to do it only to fall on my face over who discovered what when."

"Don't be silly," Sunny said. "You can't go running all over the countryside killing dragons and trolls."

"We'll never see each other again if I don't," she reasoned. "Could you be happy with the chancellor's daughter?"

Sunny sighed. "She's nice enough, but I'll never love her as much as I love you."

"Well, then, I'm on my way," Meghan said, showing more confidence than she felt.

It was almost midnight when, halfway up the mountain, Meghan came face-to-face with the dragon.

"Hello!" she said. "How are you feeling?"

The dragon, who was used to knights sneaking up

the back way, was a bit startled to find someone walking up the main road, even if that person was female, unarmored, and out of breath from the climb. "What?" he asked, scrambling to his feet.

"Oh, dear," she said. She spread her cloak on a rock and, from her pockets, took out a piece of parchment, a quill pen, and a bottle of ink. "Hard of hearing," she murmured while writing, tipping the paper to catch the moonlight. "I said," she repeated more loudly and distinctly, "How are you feeling?"

"No need to shout," the dragon answered. "I'm feeling all right. What's it to you?"

"Feeling all right," Meghan said, scribbling away. "No problems with your joints stiffening or anything?"

"No. Why?"

She didn't reply, being too busy writing down his answer. "I can't help noticing you're a bit overweight," she commented. "That doesn't affect your flying, does it?"

"Listen, little girl, you're treading on dangerous ground."

She started writing again. "Seems to have a touchy temperament," she read out loud.

"*What are you doing?*" the dragon screamed at her.

Meghan looked up, surprised. "I'm taking notes on your physical condition."

"But why?" asked the dragon.

"To know whom to bet on for the fight," she answered.

"Huh?" the dragon asked. "What fight?"

"With the giant troll," she replied.

"Now, why would I want to fight the troll?" the dragon wondered aloud.

"Because he's telling everyone you've been sitting here for too long—these are his words—on your fat behind, and he's going to come up here and take all your gold away from you."

The dragon hissed. "Let him try," he warned, smoke pouring out between clenched teeth.

Meghan pointed down the snowy mountain slope. The giant troll was pushing a huge empty wheelbarrow up the mountain path, stopping periodically to scratch his belly and yawn.

Earlier that evening, just as the sun had disappeared over the edge of the world, Meghan had awakened the troll from a peaceful sleep by sitting outside his cave and crying loudly.

"Shut up, or I'll come out and eat you!" he had

shouted from his bed. Trolls sleep during the day and are awake at night, but this was much earlier in the night than this troll was used to waking up.

Encouraged, Meghan cried even louder.

"What is the matter with you?" he warned. "Don't you know that I eat people for dinner?"

"Oh, what difference does it make?" the girl wailed. "My brothers have killed each other fighting over the dragon's gold."

"Killed each other, eh?" The troll chuckled. "And what was the dragon doing during the fight?"

"He was just lying there dead."

"Dead?" The troll was suddenly very interested.

"Oh, woe is me! All that gold—more than enough for the two of them—and now they're dead."

"The gold!" the troll called. "Is it still there?" But Meghan didn't answer. She hid behind a tree and pretended she had run away. Then she watched as the troll stopped only long enough to eat a couple of sheep and to dig his wheelbarrow out from under a pile of unwashed laundry. When he looked ready to start up the mountain to loot the dragon's den, Meghan ran ahead of him.

Now, nothing could have surprised the troll more

than seeing the supposedly dead dragon running full speed down the mountain straight at him.

"Hey!" the troll yelled. The dragon's claws reached out to crush his throat.

The troll picked up his wheelbarrow and brought it down on the dragon's head. The dragon turned around and used his spiked tail to knock over the troll.

On his way to the ground—and it was a long way for a giant troll—he pulled up a tree and jabbed the dragon in the stomach.

The dragon set the tree on fire with a blast of flame, but then got lost in the smoke. The troll took a running start toward where the smoke was thickest and bowled into the dragon.

Meghan watched the two of them tumble over the edge of a cliff.

"I'm ready for the questions now," Meghan said to the queen. The royal chancellor stood near the throne, while Sunny sat in his ceremonial chair, smiling confidently.

The queen signaled the chancellor to step forward. He still hoped his daughter would be the one to marry

Sunny and had stayed up all night helping the queen think of impossible questions.

Sunny threw kisses across the room to Meghan, who winked at him. The chancellor cleared his throat, and the royal trumpeter played his official fanfare.

Suddenly Meghan screamed, making the same sound peasants use to call the pigs: "Su-u-u-e-e-e-e-ey! Pig! Pig! Pig! Pig! Pig!" Then she dropped down to her hands and knees and made grunting noises, all the while nipping at the chancellor's ankles.

The queen stood up with her mouth hanging open.

"What's the matter with you?" the chancellor cried

Meghan jumped up. "Absolutely nothing," she answered. "Second question?"

"What?" he yelped.

"I said, 'Absolutely nothing.' Third question?"

"Wait a minute, those weren't the questions. You didn't really think those were the questions, did you?"

"Of course," Meghan snapped before the queen could say anything. "My! Those were three easy questions after all."

Sunny, who had blown a kiss after every answer, motioned the trumpeter to do another fanfare, then leaped to Meghan's side and kissed her. "My hero," he whispered.

The queen stamped her foot. "You horrible girl!" she screamed.

"You know, we have a rule in my country," Meghan said. "Anyone who is rude to the bride doesn't get an invitation to the wedding."

The queen threw her crown to the floor and wailed, "Oh, what's to become of us?"

"That's a fourth question, but I'll answer it anyway," Meghan said. "We'll probably all live happily ever after."

And she was right, for the queen calmed down and was invited to the wedding after all. The royal chancellor's daughter ran off with a juggler from the circus. And Sunny and Meghan ruled together for many peaceful years.

Carla and the Greedy Merchant

ADAPTED BY ROBERT SCOTELLARO
FROM A FOLKTALE

In the Sicilian city of Palermo, Italy, there once lived a poor shoemaker and his young daughter, Carla. The shoemaker worked with great skill creating fine leather shoes and sandals, which he sold at a nearby market. Carla helped in the shop by polishing the finely crafted shoes until they shone.

One day the shoemaker loaded his wagon with goods and hitched up his only horse.

"Wish me luck, Carla," he said. "I am going to the market and hope to return before dark with my pockets filled with coins."

Carla wished her father a speedy return, kissed his cheek for luck, and saw him on his way.

The shoemaker took a route that brought him onto a street filled with stores. As he passed by a shoe store, a wealthy merchant called to him, "Hey! Wait, my good fellow!"

The shoemaker stopped as the merchant approached.

"I see you do fine work," said the merchant, picking up a pair of leather sandals and admiring them. "Very fine indeed!" Then he looked at the shoemaker with a sly grin. "How much for everything?"

The shoemaker thought for a moment about how much he would have charged for each pair in the market and named a fair price. "Twenty copper pieces for everything."

"It's a deal!" said the merchant firmly and handed the shoemaker the coins. Then the merchant climbed onto the wagon, seated himself next to the shoemaker, and told him to step down and be on his way.

"What's this?" protested the shoemaker.

"Come now, my dear fellow, let's not quibble. You did agree to sell me 'everything,' didn't you?"

"Well, yes … but …"

"I take you at your word. Everything includes your wagon and your horse. After all, a deal's a deal! If you wish to dispute my claim, we'll go before the judge. There's one just down the street!"

In shock, the shoemaker followed the merchant to the courthouse. When they were before the judge, the merchant explained what had been said, and the judge asked the shoemaker if he had indeed agreed to sell "everything."

"Well … yes …" said the shoemaker. "But …"

"Then a deal's a deal," the judge decreed. "And you must honor it."

Dejected—without his horse, his wagon, or his pride—the shoemaker walked back home, with the cruel merchant's laugh ringing in his ears.

When he got home, he explained everything to Carla just as it happened.

"What a greedy old buzzard!" said Carla, shaking her head. "But don't worry, Papa, I have an idea."

Early the next day, Carla selected six of the finest pairs of dancing slippers the shoemaker had ever crafted.

"Let me try my luck at selling these," Carla said. Her father, seeing the determination in his daughter's eyes, consented.

Carla loaded the beautiful shoes in a wheelbarrow and was on her way. She stopped to wipe her brow when she was in front of the wealthy merchant's shop, and in a flash the merchant came running out.

"Signorina," he purred, as he approached. "You look tired. Perhaps I can relieve you of your burden!"

"That would be very nice indeed," smiled Carla.

The merchant looked in the wheelbarrow and studied the dancing slippers. "How much for everything?" he grinned broadly, thinking he would make another good deal for himself.

"How much do you offer me?" replied Carla.

The merchant reached into his pocket then held out three copper pieces. "Times are tough, Signorina. This is all I can offer."

"Everything in your hand?" Carla asked.

"Yes, certainly."

"Then it's a deal!" said Carla firmly and held out her hand for payment.

The merchant grinned slyly and slid the coins into it.

"Oh, thank you," said Carla with her hand still extended. "And I see that you have three lovely rings. I will have them as well, thank you. They are very colorful!"

The merchant was taken aback. "What's this?" he bellowed.

"Come now, my dear man, let's not quibble," said Carla. "You did agree to pay me everything in your hand, didn't you?"

Now the merchant was fuming, for he was a man prone to displaying his wealth, and on that hand he had three very valuable rings that glittered in the sunlight: a diamond, a star sapphire, and a ruby. They were among his favorite possessions.

"I take you at your word. Everything in your hand includes your three rings. After all, a deal's a deal." Carla continued, "There is a judge just down the street. If you are not content with our deal, we will go before him." And so they did.

The judge listened patiently as Carla explained what had been said. The judge asked the merchant if he had indeed agreed to pay "everything in his hand."

"Well … yes … bu—, bu—, but … ," the merchant stammered

"Then a deal is a deal," the judge decreed. "And you must honor it."

Reluctantly, the merchant slipped the beautiful rings from his fingers and handed them to Carla.

Carla put two of them in her pocket and held out the ruby ring. "I am not a heartless person," she said. "I'll bet this ring means a great deal to you."

"Why yes, it does, Signorina," said the merchant sheepishly.

"Well then, I would be willing to trade it to you for my papa's horse and wagon, which you have recently acquired," said Carla with a broad smile. The merchant, realizing he had been tricked by his own brand of trickery, agreed.

And so Carla returned home to her proud, grateful father with their horse and wagon, three copper pieces, and the two precious rings as a bonus.

Even today the people of Palermo tell of how the clever Carla outsmarted the greedy merchant.

Savannah's Piglets

ADAPTED BY SHERYL L. NELMS FROM A FOLKTALE

Just after the Civil War, when the American frontier was still being settled, few people lived on the Kansas prairies. Savannah, her mother, Liza, and her father, Jackson, were some of the first black pioneers in that Indian country. They came west in a covered wagon and bought a farm along the Blue River from the Pawnee Indians.

Jackson was a hard-working farmer who loved his wife and daughter. He'd started out working the cotton fields of Georgia as a slave but was now a free man with his own farm, planting acres of field corn in the spring and trapping red fox and mink by the river in the winter.

Liza, also a former slave from Georgia, now enjoyed keeping house, raising chickens, and growing vegetables in the garden for her own family.

Savannah enjoyed helping her mother take care of the chickens. She liked flinging golden kernels of corn around the yard for them to find. And she liked searching for plump, warm eggs in their nests. But Savannah did not like the feathers. She hated pillow-making time; that was a very sneezy job.

Savannah also helped her father with his hogs. She liked to watch the big black-and-white Poland China hogs crowd in to feed, squirming and pushing and squealing. The hogs always reminded Savannah of her cousins sitting down for Christmas dinner.

Liza, Jackson, and Savannah all worked hard. They sold their corn, hogs, furs, and chickens for good prices. They lived a good life along the Blue River, until one Wednesday morning when Liza woke up feeling nauseous.

Savannah hoped it was nothing serious—perhaps something Liza had eaten that didn't agree with her.

But that's not what it turned out to be. Liza had cholera. Many of the pioneers passing through Kansas on the Oregon Trail had been dying from cholera, and now Liza had it, too.

She died on Monday morning in the stifling August heat.

Savannah helped her father bathe and dress her mother's body in her favorite blue velvet dress. Savannah fixed her mother's hair one last time and pinned it up. She helped her father lift her mother into a homemade cottonwood coffin, then helped carry it out onto the quiet Kansas plain.

Jackson prayed a long, solemn prayer and Savannah sobbed, "Amen." They buried Liza on the tree-shaded hill behind the house.

Savannah did the best she could to help her father by cooking and cleaning, washing and mending, and feeding the chickens. She also sold their eggs and chicks and helped tend the hogs.

But that winter, Jackson grew more and more sad. Savannah tried everything she could think of to make him happy, but nothing worked.

One day, about a year after Liza had died, Jackson went to town driving his two mules with a wagonload of corn. He came home later that evening with a skinny woman in a red buggy.

"Oh, my," thought Savannah as she glanced out of the front door. "What has happened to my pa? He was so sad. Now look at him. He's smiling. He looks so happy."

Savannah could not believe her father's words when he marched into the house and began to speak. "I have found someone, Savannah. Someone to love me again. I've been so lonesome since your ma died. Now I have Billie!

"I met her this spring when I went to Marysville to buy seed corn. She came all the way from Kansas City to visit her sister. I've gotten in the habit of spending some time with her whenever I went to town. We enjoy each other's company and have decided to get married.

"I sold the corn, the wagon, the mules, the hogs, and the chickens. Now we can both go with Billie to live in Kansas City."

"I'm staying here," Savannah said without a pause. "Ma is buried here. The farm is here. This is where I belong."

"Okay, Savannah," her father replied reluctantly. "You may stay. After all you are almost a grown-up.

You can live in town in the winter, with the Ottens. In the summer, Amos Otten will stop on his way to the sawmill to check on you."

"Thank you, Pa," Savannah said, "But I wish you would stay here, too."

"Savannah," her father said, "this may be my only chance for happiness. I may not have another chance at marriage, out here in the middle of Kansas. I wish you would come with us. I love you, Savannah, but I must go."

"Goodbye, Pa. I will miss you. I love you. If you need me, I will be here. Remember me."

And so they left, but only after Billie had rifled through all of Liza's belongings. She took a trunk full of Liza's dresses, including a beautiful red dress that Savannah loved, the utensils, and all the dinnerware.

Now Savannah's father was gone, her mother was dead, and her mother's keepsakes were looted. The wagon was sold, as were the mules, the chickens, and the hogs. "All gone," Savannah thought as she looked around the empty rooms of the house her father and mother had built. "Well, at least he didn't sell the farm," she thought, glancing out the window toward the river.

A farm. Paid for by her parents after years of hard work. The land where her mother now rested. The land her father had just abandoned.

Savannah decided to hike up the hill, to visit her mother's grave. As she made her way up the path, she noticed something black moving behind the empty chicken coop. Savannah stopped still, watching.

Slowly, carefully, a mud-covered snout peeked out from behind the corner of the coop. Then another. Then another. Savannah counted ten little pig noses wiggling at her.

"Pigs!" she exclaimed. "Ten baby pigs. Where did you come from? Were you hiding down by the river? Is that where you got so muddy? My pa sold your mother and father. He sold all of your other brothers and sisters. You are orphans. Poor baby orphans." Savannah thought to herself, "We are all orphans."

Savannah glanced around the yard. What to do with the helpless piglets?

She decided the chicken coop would be best. It had worked for the chickens, and it ought to keep the pigs safe from coyotes and foxes.

"I will put you in here for now," she whispered, as

she shooed them through the open door. "At least I'll know where you are."

Once she had the pigs in the chicken coop, she sat on a fence to think. "I am all these poor little piglets have," she thought. "I must feed them. But, what will I feed them? Pa sold the corn."

Then she remembered the ears of corn still in the field—bushels and bushels of corn. Her father had sold the corn he had already harvested, but the fields were still nearly full of ripe ears. She knew what to do. She would gather the ears of corn in her mother's old bushel baskets and carry them to the pigs. Savannah knew that corn was the best food for pigs. Her father had taught her that.

She gathered heavy baskets full of corn and trudged up the hill. It was worth the effort; her little pigs ate greedily. As time went by, they grew bigger. Savannah built a fence around the chicken coop so the pigs could trot outdoors whenever they wanted to.

Meanwhile, Savannah started tending the garden. When her mother was alive, they had a huge garden. Savannah had helped plant and hoe rows of vegetables. It was hard work, but Savannah could do it.

This year her pa had planted the garden, but it had

been neglected. To get the garden back into shape, Savannah had to water it well, weed it thoroughly, and pick the vegetables. It turned out to be a good garden.

Savannah knew how her mother stored the seeds from year to year, so she dried and stored some for her own spring garden.

In October, at harvest time, Savannah had bushels of vegetables. She stored enough for herself in the cellar, then packed sacks of extra turnips and potatoes and took them to town to sell. She took six of her fattest pigs to town to sell, too. They had grown so big that there wasn't room for all ten of them in the chicken coop during the winter.

With all the money she made, Savannah bought back her father's mules. Then she filled sacks with peas and beans from her garden, tied them onto the mules, and led them to town. Savannah sold her peas and beans and bought back her father's wagon.

In November, Savannah told Mr. Otten she had to stay at the farm to take care of her mules and pigs. Somebody had to feed them. She couldn't just let them starve. He agreed and said that he would check on her from time to time. He said it looked like she was doing a pretty good job of taking care of herself and the animals and that her father would be proud of her. That made Savannah feel good, but it also made her feel sad. She missed her father. She missed her mother, too.

As winter approached, Savannah realized that the garden would not keep her busy for much longer. So, she decided to see if she could find her father's traps. When Savannah got to the shed where her father had kept his furs, she saw the rusting traps hanging at the back of the shed. She decided to use them. They were just going to keep rusting if they hung there without someone scraping and oiling them.

Savannah set her trap line through the timber along the Blue River. She had helped her pa so many times, she knew how to set the traps and cover her scent. She was happy to have something to do through the long, cold winter. Savannah was glad her mother and father had shown her how to do so much. She could build a fire, cook potato soup, bake bread, skin a rabbit, and tan a hide.

Meanwhile, in Kansas City life was not so pleasant. Billie was not the person Jackson thought he had married. She was always complaining about something. She was not as kind and cheerful as she had been when they were courting. Billie did not have a mansion, as she had claimed. Instead, she lived in a peeling, gray boarding house. Jackson had to spend half of his money to buy a decent house for them. Then Billie managed to squander the other half on frilly dresses.

By spring, Jackson was pacing the floor at night, unable to sleep. What could he do? Nothing was ever good enough for Billie. Nothing was ever fine enough. He finally decided to leave, to go back to the farm in Kansas. After all, he was a farmer. Farming was all he knew. Even when he'd been a slave in Georgia, he'd been a farmer. He could not make a decent living in the big city. He told Billie that she could come with him if she wanted, but he was leaving.

Billie decided to ride back to the farm with Jackson. He guessed that Billie just didn't want to risk losing her fringed red buggy. He wondered if she valued that buggy more than she valued him.

Savannah was furrowing the soil and planting corn when she noticed a brown dust cloud swirl down the hill. She stopped working and stood up. "It's too early for Mr. Otten," she thought. "Who could it be?"

When she finally recognized the person driving the buggy, she could hardly believe her eyes.

"Pa! Pa! Is that you? Oh, Pa, I have missed you so much," she hollered as she ran down the fence row.

"Whoa," her pa said, stopping the buggy beside the cornfield she was planting and stepping to the ground. "Savannah, I've missed you. How could I have left you? I was so foolish. I had everything I needed right here," he said, looking around at the fertile fields.

"What have you done with our farm, Savannah?" He stood there amazed. "It's beautiful! Your corn rows are so straight. Why, you're a better farmer than I am."

"Oh, no, Pa," Savannah said. "I was just trying to keep the orphan pigs fed. That was all. They needed food. I was only trying to keep us all fed."

"Well, I'm home now," he said. "I'm home to stay, if you'll let me. I'm a farmer. I belong on this land. I'm not a big-city person. I love you, Savannah. You are my daughter. Billie doesn't need me. I'm back if you'll have me for your pa again."

"Yes, Pa! Of course I'll have you!"

They both heard the crack of a whip as Billie jolted away in the buggy, its fringe flapping in the wind.

Jackson bent to hug Savannah and then looked around at the straight rows of newly planted corn. "What a good job you did, my Savannah girl! A real good job! I am so proud of you. Proud to be your pa. You saved the farm. You are my real happiness. You gave me something to come home to.

"And I have brought something back for you, Savannah girl," her father added, stepping out the front door, and returning with a suitcase. "Go ahead, open it," he said.

"Oh, Pa," Savannah gasped, after she lifted the heavy lid. "Ma's beautiful red dress! You saved it for me! Oh, thank you so much!"

Savannah and her father continued to farm along the Blue River for many prosperous years. Savannah always remembered the happiness she felt when her father returned. She also kept her mother's red dress until it was time to give it to her own daughter years later.

Kimi Meets the Ogre

An Original Story by Linda Cave

Long ago in Japan, a village lay snuggled in a valley surrounded by gently rolling hills. It was a farming village with rice fields that went up the hillsides like stair steps. Towering above the hills was a great mountain.

As in most villages, people told stories about their ancestors and how the village came to be. The storytellers spoke of a great samurai warrior who had once come to this valley and been attacked by a terrible ogre. After a long fight, the samurai defeated the ogre and sent him to live up in the mountain. Then the samurai settled down in this beautiful valley. The story had been told many, many times. No one knew for sure whether the tale was true, but whenever thunder echoed from the mountain top, the villagers said that the ogre must be stamping his feet.

Each family in the village claimed the samurai as an ancestor. One family had an old woven blanket that had, supposedly, once belonged to the samurai. Another family had a beautiful horse that was supposed to be a descendent of the samurai's horse.

But the family of Kimi and Taro had a special treasure—a giant sword in a beautifully carved wooden case. Kimi and Taro's parents said the sword had belonged to the samurai and claimed it was sharper than any knife. The scabbard for the sword was as long as their father was tall. The children had never seen anyone use the sword. In fact, they had never seen it out of its scabbard. But Kimi and Taro kept the scabbard polished until it glowed in the firelight, and all the villagers greatly admired it.

Although no one had ever seen the ogre, all the children in the village knew stories about him. When they heard thunder, they teased each other that the ogre was coming to get them. Taro not only teased his friends, but he also loved to make up scary stories about the ogre sneaking into the village while everyone was asleep. And soon all the children were repeating Taro's words.

Taro was delighted that his friends wanted to hear his stories. He began to make up more and more tales about the ogre to impress them.

One day, while he was telling one of his ogre stories, a friend asked how he knew so much about the ogre. Not wanting to admit he was just making it all up, Taro claimed he had been to the mountain and had seen the ogre. The children began to laugh. They all knew Taro had never been on the mountain. Soon they all went off to play and left Taro sitting alone.

Taro decided the only way to get his friends back to hear his stories would be to go to the mountain and find the ogre. The next morning he took a handful of rice cakes and walked up the hillside to the mountain. The sun was hot and the path up the mountain was steep. He climbed for nearly an hour before he got tired and decided to stop and eat. After his snack, Taro took a little nap. When he awoke, it was late afternoon. Taro was too scared to stay on the mountain in the dark, but he didn't want his friends to laugh at him. So he decided to go back down the mountain to the village with an exciting story. In fact, by the time he got near the village, Taro had made up a thriller.

When he arrived back in the village, Taro leaned against a tree and pretended to be out of breath from running home. It wasn't long before all the boys and the girls gathered around to hear what had happened. Taro told them about his dangerous climb to the ogre's cave. He claimed the ogre had been walking around the mountainside. As his friends' eyes grew wide, Taro kept adding to the tale, describing the ogre in terrifying detail.

"He was taller than a tree, and his footsteps shook the ground. The ogre could take a deep breath and blow down trees. He had cruel, yellow eyes as big as rice bowls. His teeth were as long and sharp as daggers. But most terrible of all were the ogre's heavy boots. With just one step, he could easily flatten a whole house."

Taro claimed he had hidden behind a huge rock and had barely escaped when the ogre saw him. He told his friends he had run all the way back to the village in hopes that the ogre would not follow him. He feared the ogre might flatten the village and smash them all. Taro was thankful to have been able to outrun the ogre and keep the village safe.

The children listened to Taro's every word. They were amazed to hear how brave he had been. All the children were amazed except Taro's sister, Kimi. She knew Taro was a good storyteller. She also knew he was not terribly brave.

The village children ran home and told their parents about Taro and the ogre. For several days, everyone told Taro how brave he was to find the ogre. They were grateful he had been able to save the village by outrunning him.

However, soon the people began to think about how terrible it would be if the ogre did come to their village. He might begin to carry off their oxen. He might even decide to carry away the villagers. What if he stomped into the village and flattened their homes? What if he blew away their rice crops? The village was not safe. Someone must drive away the ogre. But who? Why Taro, of course! Who else knew where to find the ogre? And, after all, hadn't he already saved the village from the ogre once?

The village elders came to Taro and Kimi's house. They told Taro he must go back up to the ogre's cave and drive the ogre away from their mountains. Of course, Taro knew he had never seen the ogre. In fact, as far as he knew, the ogre was just a local legend. He figured he'd go up the hill, stay there for a while, then come back and claim the ogre was gone. That would be easy.

Kimi, on the other hand, was not so sure. She suspected her silly brother had never really seen the ogre. But she was smart enough to know that if the ogre really existed, Taro would be in big trouble. So, while Taro promised to drive away the ogre the very next day, Kimi began to plan. All day the village children came to wish Taro luck. All day Kimi made preparations.

Early the next morning Taro was packed for his great adventure. All the people of the village came to see him off. With the villagers waving and smiling, Taro started walking past the fields on the hillside. Though Taro didn't know it, Kimi was packed, too. Quietly, she started out on an alternate path.

Taro walked bravely until he was out of sight of the village. His plan was to find a nice, shady place to picnic and to nap until late afternoon. Then he would go home and tell the village he had had a terrible fight with the ogre. As he walked, he began to make up a story about fighting the ogre and scaring him away. Taro was so busy thinking up his story, that he kept walking farther and farther up the mountainside. Soon he had reached a big rock standing in the path. He started around the rock to look for a place to have his meal, when he suddenly stopped.

There, on the other side of the rock, was the ogre! He was so tall that his head reached above the trees, even though he was sitting down. The ogre seemed to be enjoying the warm sun. When he opened his mouth to yawn, Taro could see that the ogre's teeth were indeed as long and sharp as daggers.

Taro just stood and stared for a whole minute. He would have run away, but he was too scared. He would have hidden behind the rock, but he couldn't move. The ogre stretched and turned toward the rock. Then he saw Taro. Taro was just about to scream for help when he heard a familiar voice behind him.

"Oh, there you are, dear brother," said Kimi. "You forgot your food. How do you expect to kill ogres on an empty stomach?"

Before Taro could even speak, Kimi bowed to the ogre.

"You didn't tell me you were going to meet small forest spirits, Taro," Kimi continued. "I am honored to meet you, little spirit."

"Small?" asked Taro.

"Little spirit?" asked the ogre.

"I must apologize for my rude brother," Kimi said to the ogre. "He is a famous warrior, and he's been asked to kill the ogre who lives on this mountain. But first he has to eat. I'm sure he'd share his food with you, but he needs all his energy to meet the big and terrible ogre."

"Famous warrior?" asked Taro.

"How big?" asked the ogre.

As Kimi talked, she pulled a large cart out from behind the rock.

"Oh, absolutely huge!" said Kimi. "Now you," Kimi turned to look at the ogre. "You seem to be a nice, polite little spirit. You'd better get away from this mountain. That awful ogre could easily stomp on you with one foot. Taro, you remember what you said about the ogre you saw up here? You said he could flatten our whole village with his boots."

"I did?" asked Taro.

"A whole village under his boots?" asked the ogre.

"Why, just last month, my brother killed an ogre who had eyes as big as rice baskets. And he says this ogre is even bigger."

"Rice baskets?" asked Taro.

"Even bigger?" asked the ogre.

"Here, Taro," said Kimi. "You'd better sit down and have your meal."

Kimi pulled a rice cake out from under the cover on the cart. It was the biggest rice cake Taro had ever seen. She could barely lift it with both arms. "You can start with this little morsel," Kimi said.

Then Kimi climbed up into the cart. She began rummaging around and making a great clatter. "Now I know I brought a knife and some jam," she mumbled.

The ogre stared at the cart as Kimi continued to dig around inside. These people were not the least bit afraid of him. In fact, they were getting ready to kill an ogre who was much bigger than he was—an ogre who could flatten him under one foot. Why, just look at the size of that rice cake. This must truly be a great warrior!

At last, Kimi stopped tossing things around in the cart. "Oh, here it is," she said. "I sharpened your *big* sword this morning. I knew you wouldn't want to use it to spread jam, so I brought this little butter knife from the kitchen. Here it is."

Then Kimi pulled back the cover on the cart.

Taro stared.

The ogre's mouth dropped open.

There, gleaming in the sun, was the samurai's sword. The huge sword as tall as a man.

"That's a butter knife?" the ogre asked. "You have a bigger sword for killing ogres?"

"Oh, of course!" said Kimi. "My brother has a tremendous, extremely sharp sword for killing ogres. This is just a dull, old kitchen knife." Then Kimi turned to face her brother, "Now, Taro, as soon as you finish eating, we can go find the ogre. Please excuse us, dear spirit … dear spirit?"

But when Kimi turned back to see the ogre, he was no longer there. The ogre was not going to wait around for Taro to get out his sword. No sir, he was going to find a mountain where he was the only ogre, the biggest ogre, far away from this ogre-killer and his sister. He hoped he'd never run into them again. And he never did.

The Innkeeper's Wise Daughter

RETOLD BY PENINNAH SCHRAM FROM A RUSSIAN FOLKTALE

One day many years ago, in a small Russian village, two friends, a tailor and an innkeeper, were drinking tea and talking about life. As their discussion went on, it became more and more heated. Each one claimed to know more about life than the other. Their voices grew louder and louder.

Realizing that they could not settle the argument by themselves, they decided to bring the dispute to a wise nobleman, who often served as a judge in such matters. The two friends finished their tea in silence and set out to see the nobleman.

When the nobleman had heard the case, he said to the two men, "Whoever answers these three questions correctly will be the one who knows more about life: What is the most powerful thing in the world? What is the fastest thing? And what is the sweetest? Return in three days' time with your answers, and I will settle your dispute."

On his way home the tailor decided on the answers to the riddles. He was confident that he had thought of the best possible answers and couldn't wait for the three days to pass.

When the innkeeper returned to his home, he was worried that he would not be able to find the right answers.

When his teenaged daughter came into the room and saw his troubled face she asked, "What's wrong, Father?"

The innkeeper told her about the three questions.

She answered, "Don't worry, Father. I will give you the answers to the nobleman's questions."

When three days had passed, the tailor and the innkeeper came before the nobleman. "Have you found answers to my questions?" he asked.

The tailor answered first. "The most powerful

thing is a horse. The fastest is an eagle. The sweetest is honey."

After the tailor had given his answers, the nobleman turned to the innkeeper.

Then the innkeeper answered. "The most powerful thing is thought. The fastest is light. The sweetest is the love of a mother for her baby."

The nobleman, waited a moment to consider their answers, and then said, "The tailor answered well. However, the innkeeper's answers were wiser."

Turning to the innkeeper, the nobleman asked, "But tell me, how did you think of those answers?"

"I must tell you truthfully that my daughter told me those answers," replied the innkeeper.

"Since your daughter knows so much about life," said the nobleman, "I will test her further. Give her these twelve eggs and ask her to hatch them all in three days. If she does so, she will have a great reward."

The innkeeper carefully picked up the eggs and returned home. That evening he showed his daughter the twelve eggs and told her what the nobleman had said. She took the eggs and noticed how heavy they were. "Dear Father, these are hard-boiled eggs! It is impossible to hatch them. But wait. I know how to answer this riddle."

The daughter boiled some beans and waited three days. Then she instructed her father to go to the nobleman's house and ask permission to plant them in the nobleman's garden.

"Beans?" asked the nobleman. "What sort of beans?"

Taking the beans from his pocket, the innkeeper showed them to the nobleman and said, "The beans I want to plant are boiled beans."

The nobleman burst out laughing and said, "Don't you know that you can't grow beanstalks from boiled beans?"

"Certainly," replied the innkeeper, "but if you think my daughter can hatch chicks from boiled eggs, perhaps you'd like me to plant these boiled beans in your garden."

From the answer the nobleman immediately realized how clever the innkeeper's daughter was. So he said to the innkeeper, "Tell your daughter to come here in three days. She must bring me a gift that is not a gift."

The innkeeper returned home even more perplexed than before.

When his daughter heard what she had to do, she laughed and said, "Don't worry, Father, I know what to do."

The next day the daughter said to her father, "Go to the marketplace and buy a nightingale." This request puzzled her father, but he loved his daughter and knew her to be wise, so he did not question her. Instead, he went to the marketplace and bought a nightingale.

On the third day, the innkeeper's daughter went to visit the nobleman. As she approached his house, the nobleman saw her and came out to greet her.

The innkeeper's daughter extended her hands, showing the songbird she intended to give as a gift. The nobleman reached out to take it, but just at that moment the young woman opened her hands and the nightingale flew away. Clearly, she had brought a gift that was not a gift.

The nobleman laughed and called out, "You are very clever indeed! I would like to marry you, but on one condition: You must promise never to interfere with any of my judgments. If you do, I will send you back to your father."

"I will marry you," said the innkeeper's daughter. "But I also have one condition: If I do anything that causes you to send me away, you must promise to give me whatever I treasure most in your house."

They each agreed to the other's condition and were married.

After some time passed, a man came to speak with the young wife, who had become known for her wisdom. "Help me, please," the man begged. "I need your advice."

"Tell me what is wrong, for you look very troubled, sir," she answered. And the man told her his story.

"My partner and I share a barn. He keeps his wagon there, and I keep my horse there. Well, last night my horse gave birth to a foal under the wagon. So my partner said the foal belonged to him. We argued and fought and then brought our dispute to your husband. Unfortunately, he judged that my partner was right. I protested, but he didn't change the decision. Now I must give the foal to my partner. What can I do?"

The young woman felt sorry for the man and gave him some advice. Following her instructions, he went to the nobleman's well with a fishing pole, put some bait on a hook, and dropped the line into the well. When the nobleman rode by the well and saw the man, he stopped and asked, "What are you doing?"

The man replied, "I am fishing in the well."

The nobleman started to laugh and asked, "Don't you know that you can't catch fish in a well?"

"Well," he replied, "if a wagon can give birth to a foal, then I can catch fish in a well."

The nobleman burst out laughing. Then he asked the man, "Tell me, how did you think of this idea?"

When the man answered, "I told my story to your wife and she took pity on me," the nobleman became very angry and went looking for his wife.

When he found her, he said, "You promised not to interfere with my judgments, but you did not keep your promise. Now I must send you back to your father's home."

"You are right, my husband," she said. "But before I leave, let us dine together one last time." The nobleman agreed to this request.

At dinner the nobleman drank a great deal of wine, for his wife kept refilling his cup. As a result he soon became very sleepy. As soon as he was asleep, the wife signaled to the servants to pick him up and put him in the carriage next to her, and they returned to her father's home.

The next morning when the nobleman woke up, he looked around and realized where he was. "How did I get here? What is the meaning of this?" he shouted.

"You may remember, dear husband, that you made an agreement with me," she answered. "You promised that if you sent me away, I would be able to take with me whatever I treasured most in your house. What I treasure most in your house is you. So that is why I took you with me."

The nobleman laughed, embraced his wife, and said, "Knowing how much you love me, I now realize how much I love you. Let us return to our home."

And they did go home, where they lived with love and respect for many happy years.

The Royal Joust

AN ORIGINAL STORY BY BRUCE LANSKY

Lady Rowena looked at the empty chair at the breakfast table and then at Lindsey. "Where is your brother? If he doesn't hurry up, he'll be late for the tournament."

"Don't worry, Mother. Reggie won't miss the finals of the Royal Joust. I'll see to that," Lindsey answered.

When she knocked on Reggie's bedroom door, Lindsey thought she heard a moan. As she opened the door, she noticed that Reggie's curtains were drawn.

He was still in bed. Stepping into the room, she realized he *was* moaning—and talking to himself.

"Oh, no! I can't move!" Reggie repeated this lament over and over.

"You can't stay in bed, Reggie. Today is the last day of the tournament, so you'd better roll your aching body out of bed and into your armor. Then ride over to North Hampton by noon, or you'll be disqualified."

"I want to, but I can't. I was sideswiped by Sir Garth's horse yesterday. I have no idea how I stayed in my saddle. Now I can't ride, I can't walk, I can't even get out of bed," explained Reggie.

"Reggie, today is the last day of the tournament, and you're still undefeated. This is your big chance. At least give it a try."

"Sorry," said Reggie, "I hate to let you down. Would you mind riding to North Hampton to tell the tournament officials I'm withdrawing from the competition?"

"No problem, Reggie. I was planning to go anyway, to watch you win. No one in the tournament has worked harder than you. I wish I could take your place and bring back a trophy for you."

"So do I!" said Reggie. "Too bad they don't let girls compete."

Lindsey thought about what he said. It bothered her that Reggie would have to drop out of the tournament on the final day. She and Reggie had been training all year. Every day, weather permitting, Reggie's page, Giles, would help them suit up in armor and hoist them onto chargers so they could joust with padded lances. Reggie was bigger and stronger than Lindsey, but Lindsey was a skilled rider, better able to guide her horse to precisely the right place at the right time. She was almost impossible to hit, let alone unseat. And Giles knew enough to keep his mouth shut about a girl learning the knightly arts.

"You don't mind if I borrow your charger for the trip, do you?" asked Lindsey.

"No problem," Reggie responded, even though it was unusual to ride a charger to town. "Lightning could use the exercise."

"Thanks, Reggie. I'll send them a message they won't soon forget."

Lindsey explained to her mother that Reggie had asked her to let the tournament officials know he was unable to compete. Then she hurried to find Giles, for without a page to help her, she couldn't put her plan into action. Giles helped Lindsey put on Reggie's suit of armor and saddle up Lightning. Together, they set off at a trot on the road to North Hampton.

Lindsey and Giles reached North Hampton just as the tournament was about to begin. The crowd milled about in a festive mood while the knights were hoisted onto their horses. No one noticed that Lindsey (disguised as Reggie) was already mounted.

Anticipation built as each contestant rode onto the field. There would be three rounds of competition with eight contestants in the first round, four in the second, and two in the third. Lindsey had drawn Sir Wilton, one of the tallest knights on the circuit, as her first opponent.

With her helmet on and her visor down, Lindsey rode past the tournament officials, dipping her lance in the traditional salute to the king and queen. Then she lined up in Reggie's place at the edge of the field, opposite Sir Wilton. Trumpets blew a fanfare, and the tournament was under way.

On the first pass, Lindsey ducked under Sir Wilton's lance and managed to strike him on the shoulder. Although Sir Wilton was stunned, he remained in his saddle.

On the second pass, Lindsey guided Lightning inside toward Sir Wilton, whose horse shied away. Sir Wilton dropped his lance as he grabbed for the reins with both hands to gain control of his horse. That's when Lindsey's lance struck him and knocked him out of his saddle.

As was the custom, Lindsey rode up to where the king and queen were seated on the reviewing stand and again lowered her lance. A murmur of surprise went through the crowd when she did not lift her visor. Lindsey didn't care; she'd made it to the second round.

Her next opponent was Sir Rockwell, last year's champion. As Lindsey lined up at the end of the field opposite him, she wondered how she could possibly unseat such a seasoned opponent. The trumpets blared and both horses galloped toward each other at breakneck pace.

Suddenly, Lindsey reigned in Lightning. The horse whinnied and dug in its heavy hooves. Sir Rockwell swung his lance away to avoid hitting Lightning, because injuring a horse meant instant disqualification. But Lindsey kept her lance trained on Sir Rockwell as he swept past her. The blow hit him squarely. He fell hard and didn't get up. Sir Rockwell seemed unconscious as his page carried him off the field, but a bucket of cold water quickly revived him.

Again Lindsey saluted the king and queen. Again she kept her visor shut. This time the crowd buzzed. People wondered why "Reggie" would not acknowledge the praise of the royal couple and the applause of the crowd by showing his face.

As Lindsey watched the other semifinalists compete, she saw Sir Gavilan unhorse his opponent in a single pass. The crowd cheered as Sir Gavilan lifted up his visor and lowered his lance to the king and queen. Clearly, he would be the crowd's favorite in the finals.

As both Lindsey and Sir Gavilan mounted their horses for the final round, he called to her, "If you won't open your visor, I'll just have to knock your helmet off."

Lindsey rode to her end of the field without saying a word. "Tongue-tied?" Sir Gavilan called out. Again, Lindsey didn't answer.

As the trumpets blared to start the final round, Sir Gavilan took off at a full gallop. But Lindsey merely trotted toward him, then stopped. Sir Gavilan was puzzled and lowered his lance. Lindsey suddenly spurred Lightning forward and would have scored a direct hit on Sir Gavilan had he not blocked her lance with his shield. He slipped to the right and almost lost his balance, but he managed to hang onto his horse with his strong legs.

Sir Gavilan's smile had been knocked off his face. He was worried as he prepared for the second pass. At the sound of the trumpets, the horses surged toward each other once again. This time, Sir Gavilan did not drop his guard. He kept his lance aimed directly at Lindsey. And even though Lindsey swerved toward him, he did not lower his lance.

Instead of trying to strike him with her own lance, Lindsey put all her strength and that of Lightning behind her shield as it met Sir Gavilan's lance. Shield crashed against lance with terrible force, and the blow knocked the lance out of Sir Gavilan's hand. It clattered, useless, to the ground.

Without a lance, Sir Gavilan had to draw his sword for the third pass; he was now at a distinct disadvantage. Bravely he drove his horse toward Lindsey, trying to get close enough to strike. But Lindsey swerved away to maintain her advantage and struck Sir Gavilan with her lance, bouncing him out of the saddle.

She had won. The tournament was over.

To a rising swell of cheers, Lindsey rode to the reviewing stand and waved to acknowledge the ovation. Without lifting her visor, she dismounted and bowed to the king and queen. The queen then presented the winner's trophy to Lindsey, who held it above her head as the crowd applauded thunderously. Then Lindsey mounted Lightning and rode around the field, holding the trophy aloft. When she returned to the reviewing stand, Lindsey handed the trophy back to the head judge so it could be engraved and happily galloped toward home.

That evening, a tournament official arrived at Lindsey's home and asked to see Sir Reginald. Lady Rowena greeted him instead, introducing herself and adding, "Reggie is in no condition to see any visitors. Please state your business to me."

"I am Sir William, head judge of the Royal Joust. I am here to present the championship trophy to Sir Reginald. His name has been engraved in silver upon it.

"I'm afraid you're mistaken, sir. Reggie had to drop out. He has been in bed all day."

Sir William was taken aback. "This is quite confusing. We all watched Sir Reginald win three jousts, unseating Sir Wilton, Sir Rockwell, and Sir Gavilan. The queen herself presented the trophy."

"Are you sure it was Reggie?" asked Lady Rowena.

"Well, he was riding the same horse he's been on all week, and wearing his usual armor — "

"But did you ever see his face?" interrupted Lady Rowena.

"Now that you mention it, Sir Reginald caused quite a stir by refusing to lift his visor before the king and queen. Rather odd, if you ask me," Sir William replied.

"Lindsey! Come here this minute!" Lady Rowena's voice rang throughout the castle. Lindsey appeared so quickly, she must have been nearby listening to the conversation.

"Lindsey, didn't you inform Sir William that Reggie was injured and would have to drop out of the tournament?"

"No, Mother, I did not."

"Did you ride to North Hampton on Reggie's horse, Lightning?"

"Yes, Mother, I did."

"You weren't, by any chance, wearing Reggie's armor, were you?"

Lindsey looked first at her mother, then at Sir William. "Yes, Mother, I was."

Lady Rowena smiled at her daughter. "Lindsey, I'm proud of you." Turning to Sir William, she said, "It is my pleasure to inform you that my daughter, Lindsey, and her brother, Reginald, have won the Royal Joust together."

"This is quite irregular! In fact, it's … it's … unheard of!" Sir William stammered.

Now it was Lindsey's turn to speak. "You would not have allowed me to compete if I had asked to take Reggie's place. So I took his place and kept my visor down so I would not be recognized."

Sir William frowned.

"Sir William, I would remind you of your duty as head judge to congratulate the winners," said Lady Rowena with a broad smile.

Sir William shook Lindsey's hand grudgingly. "By all means, congratulations are in order," he replied.

"I don't suppose you'd mind taking the trophy back and engraving Lindsey's name next to Reggie's?" Lady Rowena asked.

"Under the circumstances, I don't believe I have a choice," sputtered the befuddled judge.

Lindsey was dying to tell Reggie that they had won the Royal Joust together, but he could not be roused from a very deep sleep. So the good news would have to wait till morning.

Chardae's Thousand and One Nights

ADAPTED BY CRAIG HANSEN FROM THE
"SCHEHERAZADE" STORY IN THE ARABIAN NIGHTS

When Sultan Malik first came to power, the people of Persia rejoiced. Unlike his father, a harsh and merciless ruler, Malik listened to his subjects and often freed those he judged to be falsely accused of wrongdoing.

Many people also admired the sultan's lovely wife, Kalila, judging that it was his great love for her that aided Malik in ruling so wisely. Kalila was everything

Malik could want in a wife: a gracious hostess, a talented singer, a thoughtful advisor, and a trustworthy friend.

For seven years Malik and Kalila ruled Persia with fairness and justice. Then, in the rainy season of their seventh year, Kalila came down with a grave illness. The court doctors did what they could to save her, but nothing worked. The sickness overtook Kalila so suddenly that she died within a week of the day she first felt ill.

The sultan ordered a monument built to the memory of his beloved Kalila, and when the rainy season ended, he buried her beneath the monument in the east corner of the royal courtyard. All the people of Persia mourned with their ruler. On the night of her funeral, when he was alone at the site of her grave, Malik swore, "By Allah, I shall never love another, Kalila, as I have loved you."

A full year passed as the sultan mourned for his dead wife. Each day he spent hours sitting beside her grave. He began to neglect his official duties and became short-tempered with those who came before him seeking justice.

The people of Persia grew worried, for Kalila had never given birth to an heir. In spite of this, the sultan showed no signs of wishing to marry again. Finally Jamal, the grand vizier and the sultan's most trusted advisor, confronted Malik.

"O Great Sultan, rule forever," Jamal said. "If I may be so bold, do you not think it is time to take a new wife?"

"Why should I take a new wife?" Malik asked, his voice weary and bitter. "The woman I loved is dead. Who could ever replace her?"

"This is not just about you, Malik. You are the sultan. The people expect you to produce a wise and benevolent heir who will follow in your footsteps."

At this Malik grew agitated, but he understood the value of Jamal's advice. "Perhaps you are correct. Seek out a new wife for me. I shall give you one year. But be forewarned: I will do this for my people, for I can never love again."

So Jamal set out on a journey across the great land of Persia in search of a woman who could please the still-grieving sultan. He talked to many women, all of whom were eager to marry the sultan. When a year had passed Jamal returned with the woman he felt would most please Malik.

"O Great Sultan, rule forever," Jamal said with a flourish. "I have completed my journey and behold, I present to you Rihana, daughter of Salim, your most faithful subject in the mountains to the north."

When Rihana entered, Malik was amazed, for she looked exactly like Kalila. "You have served me well, Jamal," Malik said. "Let the wedding preparations begin."

Now, it was the custom of the land that if a wife displeased her husband, he could divorce her by simply telling her so three times. Such women were then forced to return to the house of their fathers in disgrace, unable to marry again. For as long as anyone could remember, no sultan had ever divorced his wife, because it brought great shame not only on the woman, but on the royal throne as well.

But on the night of their wedding, Malik asked Rihana to sing him a song before bedtime, just as his beloved Kalila had done. "I am sorry, but my singing is so poor, I am afraid it will offend your ears," Rihana said.

At this, Malik became angry and told Rihana, "I divorce you."

The next day, Malik invited some visitors from a

distant kingdom to a great party thrown in their honor. But when they arrived, Rihana did not greet them in the accustomed manner; no one had ever taught her the fine points of court etiquette. Again the sultan grew angry and, in front of his guests, told Rihana, "I divorce you."

Soon afterward, when Malik told Rihana he had to leave the court for a few days to supervise the defense of a province that had been attacked by enemy forces, she blurted out, "Please do not leave me."

Malik then knew he had made a mistake and told his wife, "You are a bad advisor, for you put your own needs ahead of those of the people of Persia." Then, for the third time he said, "I divorce you. Go, return to the house of your father." And so she did.

The next day Malik met with the grand vizier and was greatly displeased. "How could you disappoint me so? Rihana may have looked like Kalila, but she possessed none of her talents. Go find me a better wife."

So once again Jamal searched throughout the land for a woman who would please the sultan. At the end of a year he returned with another young woman.

"O Great Sultan, rule forever. I present to you

Medina, daughter of Khalil, your most faithful servant in the southern desert. She has been well-schooled in the duties of the wife of a sultan."

Medina also bore a strong resemblance to the sultan's first wife, and so they were wed soon thereafter. As the days passed, Medina seemed to live up to Malik's high expectations. She was a gracious hostess and proved to be a wise advisor. An entire month had passed, and although Malik did not love his new wife, he began to trust her. One night, after she had finished singing to him, Malik told Medina, "Please, check the room for snakes."

Medina checked the room, and finding none, reassured the sultan he had no cause for concern. But he told her, "Tell this to no one, for I do not wish others to think I fear snakes."

Medina agreed, but the very next day the sultan found her discussing the matter with Jamal. Malik burned with rage. He stared harshly at Medina and shouted, "I am betrayed! Medina, I divorce you, I divorce you, I divorce you. Now go, return to the house of your father."

Medina fled the palace in tears. Jamal confronted the sultan immediately. "O Great Sultan, rule forever.

You know the law says a man can have only four wives. Already you have had three. You cannot keep divorcing every woman I bring you."

"Who shall stop me?" Malik demanded, for his heart had grown cold. "I am the sultan. I make the laws. If I wish to marry every woman in the kingdom and divorce them all, I shall. Now go, find me a new wife."

As Jamal left the palace to prepare for his journey, his heart grew heavy. He believed no woman could ever win the sultan's heart. And so it was that word of the sultan's foul temper spread throughout Persia faster than the grand vizier's camel could carry him. And no woman would agree to marry the sultan because they all feared him.

Now, the grand vizier had two daughters of his own. The youngest, Dayana, was a simple young woman who enjoyed the ordinary tasks and pleasures of daily life and had no desire to live in a palace. But the grand vizier's oldest daughter, Chardae, was not only beautiful and wise, but as independent as the wind. Several years ago she had run away to see the world.

So it was that when Jamal returned from his unsuccessful journey to find the sultan a fourth wife, he was greeted at the door by Dayana and Chardae who had recently returned from her travels. "Daughter, you have returned to me," Jamal said joyfully when he saw her. He embraced her warmly. "Have you now come to your senses and given up your rebellious behavior?"

Chardae responded with a smile. "Father, you are the one who called me rebellious. I told you when I left that I wanted to see the world, and so I did. What is wrong with that?"

"But traveling alone is not allowed for a woman."

"It's a silly rule," Chardae said. "Furthermore, I dressed as a man and traveled with a group of storytellers. I was never alone. Father, the sights I saw and the stories I could tell you of far-off lands and strange peoples would hold you spellbound many a night. But I can see you still do not approve, so I shall speak of it no more. I am not here to argue with you."

"Then what has brought you back to me, little one?" Jamal asked.

"Word of the death of the sultan's wife and the troubles it has brought the people of Persia reached me. How does the sultan fare?"

And so Jamal told his oldest daughter of his difficulty in finding the sultan a suitable wife. As he finished, he said, "And now I have failed in my duty to find someone enough like Kalila to please Malik."

"Perhaps that is the reason for your failure, Father. I knew Kalila. She was her own person. No one could ever begin to match her."

"Then what hope is there?" the grand vizier exclaimed.

"Do not worry," Chardae replied. "I shall marry the sultan."

"Have you lost all of your senses?" Jamal shouted. "You are nothing like his first wife! He'll divorce you in an instant and then you shall be disgraced, just as the women before you have been."

"Do not be troubled, Father. I have a plan. I returned to this land with the hope of marrying Malik. I have had enough traveling for one lifetime. Now I wish to marry."

"Then marry another. Marry someone who will not divorce you and leave you in dishonor."

But Chardae would not be swayed. "I do this not only for myself, Father, but for the women of Persia. You have told me of the sultan's vow to marry and divorce every woman in the land. I cannot allow him to bring such dishonor to my sisters."

When Jamal realized he could not persuade Chardae to drop her plan, he said, "Very well. You are as stubborn as ever, but since I have no other bride to offer, I will present you to the sultan tomorrow. But, please tell me your plan."

"In a moment, Father. First, there is something I must ask of my sister." Chardae turned to her. "Dayana, will you agree to help me with my plan at the wedding and afterward? Otherwise, I may fail."

Dayana agreed eagerly. She had sorely missed her sister in the years that Chardae had been traveling and did not wish to see her dishonored. So Chardae explained her plan to avoid the sultan's wrath.

The next morning Jamal entered the court of the sultan, who was in a foul temper. "You have been gone for a year, Jamal," Malik said without the pretense of formality. "Have you found me a new wife?"

"O Great Sultan, rule forever," Jamal said politely. "I present to you my own daughter, Chardae."

Malik was shocked. As the grand vizier's daughter entered the court, Malik shouted, "Are you mad,

Jamal? Have you forgotten my vow never to love again? Your daughter will be dishonored before the sun sets!"

But before Jamal could reply, Chardae spoke up. "Sultan, it was my choice to marry you. If I do not please you, I will accept your decision."

Malik glared at her. "No woman alive can please me. You would be better off to tie a millstone around your neck and jump into the sea."

Chardae's composure was not shaken. "No matter how hopeless it may be, I still wish to marry you."

"Very well," Malik said. "We shall be wed this very day."

And so it was. That night, after the wedding, Dayana was still helping her sister move in when Malik entered the room. He ordered Dayana to leave, but she begged a favor of the sultan.

"O Great Sultan, rule forever," Dayana said. "I ask only one thing. My sister has been away quite some time. Before I leave her, please grant that I may hear some of the tales of her travels and the people she encountered."

The sultan thought about this. "I see no harm in it," he said. "Very well. If Chardae is willing, she may speak of these travels."

"I am willing, dear husband," Chardae replied. And so she began to tell a fascinating tale about a peasant boy and a magic lamp. Dayana listened with great pleasure, and as the tale grew in excitement, even the sultan was anxious to hear what happened next. But just as the tale reached the most exciting moment, Chardae yawned.

"I grow weary," she said. "I will have to finish this tale another time."

"But I must know how it ends," Malik insisted.

"I am truly sorry, dear husband, but I cannot keep my eyes open a minute longer."

"Very well," Malik allowed.

On the second night, when she finished the tale of the magic lamp, both the sultan and Dayana applauded. "You must tell another," Dayana insisted, and the sultan agreed.

This time, Chardae told the tale of a young man who discovered a carpet that could fly and take him on incredible journeys across great distances. Once again, just as the story was at its most suspenseful moment, Chardae yawned and insisted she must sleep before continuing her tale.

"All right," Malik said. "But you must promise to

tell me how it turned out tomorrow night."

On the third night, Chardae finished her tale and this time it was the sultan himself who demanded to hear another. So Chardae began a third tale about a smart young lad who outwitted forty thieves. And again, at the most exciting moment, Chardae begged to be allowed to rest, and the sultan agreed.

And so it went, night after night. Each time Chardae finished a tale, Dayana or the sultan insisted she tell another. And each time the story reached its most exciting point, Chardae would stop for the night.

As the days passed, Chardae faced many situations in which her diplomatic skills as a sultan's wife were tested. Some of the time she succeeded brilliantly, surpassing even Malik's expectations. At other times she fell short, not being as well-trained in the art of ruling as Kalila had been. Whenever Chardae failed, Malik would take her aside and say, "I would be well within my rights to divorce you." But then he would remember the tale Chardae had told the night before, and he would be so anxious to learn the outcome, he would forgive her.

Time passed and Chardae made fewer and fewer mistakes, until her skill at aiding Malik in ruling surpassed that of Kalila. Soon Malik took to asking Chardae to repeat some of her tales to visitors from foreign lands. News of the sultan's wife and her fascinating tales spread throughout the world. But not once did she ever repeat a tale she had not yet finished telling to Malik. The stories Chardae told lasted for a thousand and one nights. When she finished her final tale, Malik said, "Time has proven you, Chardae. You are nothing like my beloved Kalila, but I have come to love you nevertheless. Let us produce an heir to signify our love." And so they did.

For the rest of his days the sultan ruled with fairness and justice, just as he had done in his youth. And so it was that the kingdom of Persia was saved. The sultan's wife, Chardae, came to be known as Scheherazade, which means "savior of her people." The tales she told were written down and came to be known as *The Arabian Nights*.

Lian and the Unicorn

An Original Story by Vivian Vande Velde

Long ago, Lian lived in the Chinese emperor's palace and helped her parents prepare food in the imperial kitchens. In all of her fourteen years she had never met the prince.

Oh, she'd caught an occasional glimpse of him here and there and could see he was handsome and always surrounded by friends and attendants. And she'd certainly helped prepare food for his many parties and banquets. But unlike the emperor, who made a point of thanking the kitchen staff at the beginning of the New Year festival, or the empress, who gave the palace servants presents on their birthdays, the prince was always too busy to come to the kitchen.

That was why Lian was surprised to see him one spring afternoon when she was out in the meadow collecting flowers and blossoms for the emperor's dinner table.

As he walked closer to her, Lian could see that the prince was even more handsome than she had thought. He wore a fine silk robe woven in red thread for happiness and a silk jacket embroidered with dragons. Suddenly she was very conscious of the grass stains on the knees of her simple servant's robe and of the way her hair was coming loose from its braid.

"Your Imperial Majesty," she greeted the prince, bowing low.

The prince put a finger to his lips, but then shook his head. "Too late," he said.

"Too late for what, Your Majesty?" Lian asked, bowing again.

"A deer was standing at the edge of the trees," the prince explained. "It ran away when you spoke."

Lian nodded. "Many animals come to the meadow when I'm working quietly—badgers, squirrels, deer — "

" — And unicorns?" interrupted the prince.

"Yes," Lian said, surprised that he had asked.

"I've never seen a unicorn," the prince said. "No matter how quiet I am."

"Ah," Lian said. "That's because unicorns don't like quiet. They like music."

"Music? What do you mean?"

Lian put down her basket of flowers and reached into the sleeve of her robe. She pulled out the little wooden flute the empress had given her on her tenth birthday. Then she sat down on the soft grass and played a gentle tune.

"That's very pretty," the prince said as he sat down next to her. "Continue."

"But I have flowers to gather and pots to scrub and …"

The prince waved airily. "Someone else can do that. Play."

He was, after all, the prince, so Lian played. And played. And played. Until suddenly she heard the prince take in a sharp breath.

Lian looked up and saw a unicorn peeking out from between two trees on the edge of the meadow. "Continue," the prince whispered.

Lian kept playing, and the unicorn came closer—closer than any unicorn had ever come to her before. Lian decided the reason was that her music sounded so happy. After all, she was sitting here in the meadow next to the prince himself.

The unicorn came closer still. Lian caught her own breath in amazement and almost missed a note, for up close the creature was more beautiful than she had imagined. It was the size of a small horse, pure white, with a horn that looked as much like gold as anything she'd seen in the palace. And its eyes were green, the color of jade—she saw that clearly, because the unicorn was looking directly at her.

"Keep playing," the prince told her, his voice the barest whisper.

The unicorn tossed its head and stamped its feet as though nervous, but still it came closer, until it stood right before Lian and the prince. Then the unicorn lay down in the grass at their feet, listening to Lian's music, smelling of wildflowers. Lian could not resist the urge to reach out and pet it. Its mane was as soft as it looked. The unicorn shivered but otherwise remained motionless.

Lian caught a glimpse of some people watching at

the edge of the meadow. Before she could ask him who they were, the prince said, "Keep playing. They are my attendants."

Lian couldn't understand why so many of the prince's servants were nearby. She looked back at the prince and saw that he now held a length of rope, which he had kept concealed in his jacket pocket.

Lian took the flute from her lips. "No," she said, even though she was talking to the emperor's son. Suddenly, the flute felt like ice in her hands.

But it was too late. The prince dropped a loop of rope around the unicorn's neck. But the unicorn still didn't move and looked only at her.

"Thank you," the prince said to her, as though she had wanted to help.

"I'm sorry," Lian whispered, bending forward to the unicorn's ear. Did unicorns understand human speech? She found the courage to glare at the prince.

"You won't harm it, will you?" she asked, feeling guilty about her role in the capture.

"Of course not," the prince said. "I want to build a zoo. It will have one of every species of bird and animal that lives in my father's empire. But the unicorn will be my most prized attraction."

Lian thought the unicorn looked much better in the meadow than it ever would in a zoo. "I'm sorry," she told the creature again.

"You're being silly," the prince snapped as his men came out from hiding among the trees and gathered around him.

They congratulated him and shouted "Well done!"—a compliment Lian did not think he deserved.

Then the prince tried to leave, but the unicorn wouldn't get up, no matter how hard the prince tugged on the rope.

When she saw that the prince wouldn't give up, and the unicorn would get hurt, Lian bowed and said, "Your Majesty, allow me."

The unicorn got to its feet when she took the rope. As she led the unicorn through the woods and back toward the palace, Lian thought about the prince. Now that she had finally met him, she was sorely disappointed.

The prince was so delighted with the unicorn, he gave Lian's family three gold pieces. Together with the money her parents had been saving, they had enough to retire from the imperial kitchens and buy a tea-house near the palace.

"You must visit the palace every day," the prince commanded Lian. Lian realized he didn't want her to visit him; he only wanted her there to tame the unicorn.

Day after day, Lian walked from the teahouse to the palace. Day after day, she watched the prince harness the unicorn to a specially designed wagon that he would ride in so people throughout the land could admire him and gape at his unicorn. Day after day, she grew angrier.

One day the prince was out until after dark. Watching from the shadows, Lian noticed that the unicorn was covered with mud and could barely walk. As the prince unhitched the wagon and led the tired unicorn to its pen, Lian thought, "Unicorns are the symbol of wisdom; this prince is foolish."

Once the stableboy locked the unicorn in its pen and returned the key to the prince, Lian came out and stood by the gate. As soon as the unicorn saw her, it raised its tired head and stood proudly for her.

Lian knew what she had to do. She climbed over the wall. It was high enough to keep a horse from getting out, but as everyone knows, a unicorn is very different than a horse.

She jumped down into the pen, and the unicorn immediately came over to greet her. "You poor creature," Lian said. "I'm here to rescue you."

The unicorn looked at the gate. "Maybe it *can* understand me," she thought. But when she said, "I don't have the key. You'll have to jump the wall," the unicorn didn't seem to understand her. It didn't look at the wall; it only looked at her.

Lian gently took the unicorn's head in her hands and turned it in the direction of the wall. "Jump," she said, making shooing motions.

Instead, the unicorn got down on its knees and gently nuzzled her leg.

Was the unicorn inviting her to get on its back?

Being a kitchen servant, Lian had never ridden on a horse. Nevertheless, she climbed on the unicorn's back, her arms securely around its neck, and whispered "Ready" in its ear.

Carefully, the unicorn got up on its feet and slowly circled the pen, allowing Lian to get used to its gait. It circled faster and faster. Suddenly, they were galloping at full speed toward the wall. Lian held on tight and closed her eyes. Then they were off the ground flying over the wall. After what seemed an impossibly long time, they hit the ground, still running, and gradually slowed down. They were on the other side.

Lian thought they'd head for the forest. But the unicorn circled around to the back of the palace instead, to the smaller pens and cages where the prince kept the animals he'd captured while his zoo was being built.

"Of course," Lian thought. "They need to be rescued, too." As the unicorn walked up to the nearest cage, Lian leaned over and unhooked the latch. The cages were not locked because the prince wasn't worried about anyone stealing common animals. The unicorn walked her around the courtyard as she leaned over to unfasten the latches and open every cage. She released a panda, a tree shrew, a tiger, a fox, a goat, and three different kinds of monkeys. Instead of running away, the animals waited for her to finish opening the rest of the cages.

Once Lian set free all the animals, the unicorn led them to the edge of the forest. Even the birds didn't stray far ahead, but kept circling back to keep pace with the easily distracted rabbit. Only when they were under cover of the forest did the animals finally scatter silently.

Lian slid off the unicorn and gave it a hug. The unicorn rested its head against her shoulder. "It was a wonderful ride," she said. "But you need to go. As everyone knows, unicorns are meant to be free."

The unicorn looked at her one final time with those beautiful jade-colored eyes, turned, and disappeared into the darkness between the trees.

No one ever suspected Lian, the teahouse owner's daughter, of helping the imperial zoo animals to escape. After all, the gate to the unicorn's pen was still locked, and only unicorn tracks were visible among the opened zoo cages. Obviously, unicorn magic was involved. Everyone blamed the prince for having kept the unicorn out all day and away from Lian. They figured her taming effect had worn off.

The prince, who—like the rabbit—was easily distracted, never did resume work on his zoo.

And no one ever seemed to notice that in the early morning dew, unicorn tracks were sometimes visible on the grass between the new teahouse and the forest. Some tracks were light, the way unicorn tracks usually are, but some were deeper, heavier, almost as though the unicorn carried a rider.

But as everyone knows, no one can ride a unicorn ....

AUTHOR BIOGRAPHIES

Linda Cave is a former elementary-school teacher. She has worked as an editor for several educational publishers and is currently a freelance writer and editor. She has contributed poems and stories to a number of educational programs.

Craig Hansen holds an M.A. in Creative Writing from Mankato State University and runs Rose Creek Publishing, an electronic publishing company in Saint Paul, Minnesota. In 1989, he received a first place award for college investigative journalism from the Minnesota Newspaper Association. Hansen's novel, *She Gives at the Office,* is currently being serialized in *Whispering Pines Quarterly.*

Bruce Lansky enjoys writing stories and funny poems for children (his most popular poetry books are *Kids Pick the Funniest Poems, A Bad Case of the Giggles,* and *The New Adventures of Mother Goose*), and he loves to perform in school assemblies and workshops. Before he started to write children's books, Lansky wrote humorous books for parents and baby name books. He has two grown children and currently lives with his computer near a beautiful lake in Minnesota.

Sheryl Nelms graduated from South Dakota State University and has published over 3,500 articles, poems, and short stories. She was born in Marysville, Kansas, and researched the history of that area while writing her story for *Girls to the Rescue.* Nelms is currently working as an insurance adjuster in Fort Worth, Texas.

Peninnah Schram is a storyteller, teacher, recording artist, author, and an associate professor of speech and drama at Stern College of Yeshiva University. She is also the founding director of the Jewish Storytelling Center in New York City, the author of numerous books of Jewish stories, and the editor of *Chosen Tales: Stories Told by Jewish Storytellers.*

Robert Scotellaro has published his poetry and fiction in over one hundred anthologies, literary magazines, chap books, and children's magazines, including *Highlights.* He is also the author of *Daddy, Fix the Vacuum Cleaner,* published by Willow Wisp Press. Scotellaro was born in Manhattan, New York, and now lives in San Francisco, California, with his wife, Diana, and five-year-old daughter, Katie.

Vivian Vande Velde is the author of seven books for children and a number of short stories published in magazines such as *Cricket* and *Highlights.* She is currently living in Rochester, New York, with her husband, daughter, cat, rabbit, and hamster.

Girls to the Rescue, Book #2

Edited by Bruce Lansky

Here is the second groundbreaking collection of folktales featuring ten clever and courageous girls from around the world. Among the heroes in this book you will meet Jamila, a girl who saves her village from a terrible lion; Adrianna, a Mexican girl who rescues her family's farm from ruin; and Vassilisa, a Russian aristocrat who saves her brother from prison. (Ages 8-12.) **$3.95**

Girls to the Rescue, Book #3

Edited by Bruce Lansky

The runaway success of the *Girls to the Rescue* series continues with this third collection of folk tales from around the world, featuring such heroic girls as Emily, a girl who helps a runaway slave and her baby daughter reach safety and freedom; Sarah, a Polish girl who saves her father from prison; and Kamala, a Punjabi girl who outsmarts a pack of thieves. (Ages 8–12) **$3.95**

Young Marian's Adventures in Sherwood Forest

by Stephen Mooser

In the tradition of *Girls to the Rescue,* this novel-length story tells the exciting tale of spunky, 13-year-old Maid Marian. With the help of young Robin of Loxley, the future Robin Hood, Marian battles a pack of hungry wolves and outsmarts murderous thieves and the Sheriff of Nottingham while trying to save her father from the hangman's noose and solve the mystery of her missing mother. **$4.50**

Perform a *Girls to the Rescue* Play!

Now you can produce *Girls to the Rescue* plays at school using scripts and materials from Baker Plays. Please call (617) 482-1280 for more information.

Also from Meadowbrook Press

✦ **Free Stuff for Kids**
The number one kids' activity book! Published yearly, with hundreds of free and up-to-a-dollar offers children can send for through the mail, including stickers, crafts, hobbies, and Internet offers.

✦ **Long Shot**
Eleven-year-old Laurie Bird Preston leaves her town, friends, and basketball teammates behind when her father takes a job in another city. Laurie faces a new team with new challenges, but discovers that with time, understanding, and help from a quirky kid named Howard, being happy may not be such a long shot. *Available Fall 2001.*

✦ **Newfangled Fairy Tales Series**
A series of entertaining fairy tales with delightfully newfangled twists on classic stories and themes, providing contemporary settings that will appeal to both boys and girls.

✦ **Troop 13: The Mystery of the Haunted Caves**
Becca and her three best friends are determined to win the gold medal at the scouts' Gold Rush Jamboree. And when they find a mysterious map hinting at treasure buried nearby, they're determined to find it, too, even if it means sneaking from camp, exploring bat-filled caves, and risking their safety when robbers threaten them.

We offer many more titles written to delight, inform, and entertain.

To order books with a credit card or browse our full selection of titles, visit our web site at:

www.meadowbrookpress.com

or call toll-free to place an order, request a free catalog, or ask a question:

1-800-338-2232

Meadowbrook Press • 5451 Smetana Drive • Minnetonka, MN • 55343